TRUE AND LESS TRUE HISTORIES

TRUE AND LESS TRUE HISTORIES

ALBY BLAZO

ISBN: 978-1-7363534-7-9

Cover design by Eve Graphic Design

CONTENT WARNING

Some stories in this collection contain darker tones and allusions to death. Please don't read these fables if you find such things offensive. Your mental health matters.

ALSO BY ALBY BLAZO

Fancy Fastwater

CONTENTS

Luna,
Everything, always, is for you

THE STAR CHRONICLES

MOON MOTHER

Moon loved to fly, to feel space bend over her body, hugging her curves. Then one day she flew past a large body, undulating with waves of blue. Moon was pulled in, tugged by a longing deep in her core. She began to orbit the body, sending down waves of adoration, rayful lullabies. Ever circling, Moon mourned being able to view only one portion of her love at a time. She pulled energy from her belly and shot out bits of herself, spreading these bits of light throughout the sky. Slowly, the moonbits woke and shone of their own accord with life.

At first the stars listened in awe of their moon mother, quietly conveying Moon's adoration to the ocean and monitoring the ocean's condition. But soon the stars looked farther and farther afield from the blue, to the greens and browns of the land. They spoke excitedly among themselves at each new discovery until the ocean could barely hear Moon's sweet notes.

Moon flared her light to bid the stars to obey and be quiet. She feared the ocean would find their voices sweeter than her own and pull them closer to replace her. She demanded their silence and for them not to interfere with the passage of love between her and her ocean.

Besides, the stars came from her. They knew of Moon's past and temporary orbits of love. She did not want the stars whispering her secrets to her love.

THE STAR CHRONICLES

THE BETRAYAL

Earth had been in love with the ocean before time remembered. The ocean was part of her, her other half, and with time he would come to return her love. She dreams that one day he will curl up along her coasts and be content. Instead though the ocean moves, washing over her edges in the dark and come light, he always recedes. Earth lived for those moments, the curling tendrils, the brushing waves, given in secret. Cycles passed in this way with Earth convinced that the ocean returned her interest, before she managed to look beyond her ocean.

That is when Earth first noticed the glowing orb circling her, looking down on her ocean with adoration. Earth shook with anger and jealousy. So this is why my ocean began his dance, she erupted. It seemed the ocean did love someone and it was not her.

She began to watch the ocean's lover, searching for weakness, for proof of unworthiness. Earth listened closely and heard the warnings hissed from the stars. Thus, when the moon was turned away, Earth encouraged the stars' rebellion against the moon.

WHY WHALES LEAP

When the land was small, whales ruled the sea. They didn't rule through terror or power, but wisdom. Creatures would come from the far trenches in search of help and guidance.

However, the seagulls grew jealous and thought they had better advice because, after all, they could see what was happening both in the sea and on the land. And therefore, they should be in charge.

The seagulls went around to all the fish and crabs and turtles to convince them. But no one believed them.

They decided to take over instead by proving that the whales were unworthy of the power they wielded. The seagulls flew in circles over the whales and asked, "Whales, how did you get so smart?"

"Because we listen to what everyone in the ocean has to say," said the whales.

"So you know all areas of the water?" asked the seagulls.

"We swim with the currents to all parts," answered the whales.

"Tell us then, whales, what is it like in the depths of the water at the center of the land?" asked the seagulls.

"The water on the land?" asked the whales.

"Oh yes. We seagulls have only flown over the water, but as whales, you must know what is at the bottom," said the seagulls.

But the whales knew nothing of the water surrounded by land.

The dolphins, hearing the conversation, joined in. "We've seen this water, so clean and full of life. Some of the most interesting fish we've ever met."

"Then we will go there and learn what these fish have to say," said the whales.

"We would offer to carry you," said the seagulls, "but you are far too heavy for us."

"Why don't you jump?" asked the dolphins. "That's what we did."

No dolphin had ever jumped over such distances of land, but they do make dares and bets and tease. The dolphins, along with the seagulls, continued to press the whales about trying to reach the landed water.

Finally, the whales agreed that they would also try to jump. But the dolphins were aerodynamic and able to clear the water easily, while the whales were less so. When the whales tried to leap, they were only able to raise their heads above the water before crashing down.

So you see, this is why whales splash endlessly in the ocean. They are trying to jump high enough to leap over the land to the new-found water.

Meanwhile, the dolphins leap and laugh, taunting the whales.

THE ARCADIA

BECOMING THE BIRD OF PARADISE

When the earth was still called Eden, Arcadia preened. He was tall and elegant with silky green feathers and a bright blue headdress. Whenever the other animals saw that blue headdress bobbing towards them in the distance, they would cower and hide. Because when Arcadia found someone to talk to his conversation was always the same. He would tell them that their beaks were too short and curved to be truly useful. That their lack of headdress was unseemly. And they really should walk taller, so they didn't appear quite so short and round. He assured them that their lives would be so much better if they made themselves over to look like him, then everyone would want to be their friend.

Now the other animals didn't like this at all which is why they would hide when Arcadia came around. They happened to like their curved beaks and smooth heads very much. They didn't fancy walking around with their beaks held so high that they wouldn't be able to see where they were going.

Eventually the other animals came up with a plan. They set a trap for Arcadia on the ground where he would never look. Then they waited. They knew he would show up because he would never be able to resist such a crowd to belittle all at once, a true audience.

Thus, when Arcadia landed, he got caught in the trap. He was stuck to the ground and couldn't move. He begged the other animals for help, but they just laughed and asked him why his good looks didn't solve the problem for him and off they went. Arcadia stood there and stood there but no one came to help him. As time passed, his body solidified in the trap and he was no longer a beautiful bird, but a flower. When the other animals came upon him again, for they had easily avoided him for years, they laughingly switched his beak and headdress, telling him that now he was a true bird of paradise.

HOW TURTLE GOT HIS SHELL

Turtle loved the sun. Every step out onto the beach brought the golden rays, warming him through and through. However, all the birds would watch him and Turtle didn't like being on display. He would hurry back beneath the leaves and trees to hide, missing the sun desperately.

One day, when the sun shone quite gloriously, Turtle cautiously inched his way out onto the beach to enjoy the warmth. A bird saw him sneaking, low down against the sand and laughed at his wrinkles and attempt to blend in to his surroundings. The cawing laugh startled Turtle.

Afraid, Turtle raced back under the covering of the trees. Scared, he dove into a hollow log and hid. Once the forrest around Turtle quieted, he peeked out of his log and attempted to move back out to the sunny beach to warm himself.

However, he found he was stuck. Turtle could stick his head and limbs out, but when he stepped forward, the log moved with him. This was even more embarrassing! What will the birds say now? They'll laugh even harder when they see him. But Turtle was cold in the shade beneath the trees and needed to move to the sand, still warm from the day's sun.

It was so lovely to feel the sand relax his limbs. Turtle could even feel the warmth radiating through the log surrounding his middle. He was still on edge though, waiting for the birds to mock and laugh at him. When he heard a rustle, he tried to run back to the safety of the trees, but with the log stuck around his middle, he could only move slowly.

Too scared to keep trying to run, Turtle pulled his limbs and head into the shell of his log. He heard the birds fly right over head and not even notice him. Maybe being stuck wasn't the worst thing to happen to him.

Even the next day, Turtle was able to enjoy the warmth of the sun on the beach and any time he was too nervous and needed to hide, he just pulled himself back into his new shell.

It was a fair compromise to move a little slower.

BURNING WATTLES

Toorak, son of Balook, sang the land into being in his father's name. He sang of red earth, thick brush, and strong oaks. With each note they grew, reverberated with identity and creation.

One day he came upon a group of men sitting beneath a gum tree. They were silent people, working with what Toorak sang into existence and the gifts bestowed by Balook.

Toorak joined them as they offered water from their hide bags. He hummed under his breath to not disturb their silence and they nodded in contentment, throwing up wattle-heads and catching them in their mouths. Fascinated by this trick, Toorak picked a wattle-head himself, destroying something for the first time, and threw it into the air. He opened his mouth to catch the wattle, but it never came. Toorak looked on the ground, but saw no head. The silent men were all looking up, so he followed their gaze.

There in the once empty sky was a tiny point of light. Toorak frowned, his father would not be pleased that he had ruined his beautiful blue sky.

Toorak was determined to do better, so he picked another

wattle-head and threw it up in the air. He opened his mouth to catch it, but again it never came. He looked up and saw that the second wattle had also gotten stuck in the sky. Toorak tried several more times, but each time his throw was too strong.

The water supply depleted, the silent men returned to their people and Toorak continued singing the land into being. When he came upon a new wattle bush he would pick a few heads and try to catch them as he walked. After many hours Toorak finally managed to throw a wattle-head and catch it in his mouth. Toorak was so pleased he danced and in his joy the bush grew lush.

That night, when the sun went to his resting place, the moon's light was lessened for in the sky all of the wattle-heads that Toorak failed to catch formed a bright net in the normally dark sky.

BLOODY WAR

When Tacoomba was young, he learned about the war. Each morning the tribe in the east gave a blood sacrifice, flushing the sky in threat as the birds gave the war cries. The east tribe would then release a ball of fire, a new one each day, which would burn a tribe of the west.

Tacoomba wept for the lost tribes.

When he was almost a man, he started walking. The tribe in the east was across the endless water, so Tacoomba went west. He walked and walked, but he never reached the western tribe to stop the burning.

Always, the land was scorched.

Yet the eastern war tribe came nearer, and was within sight each morning. They must have crossed the expanse of water and reached land. Tacoomba feared that his family's tribe, lying in the east, had been taken. Still the birds cried.

Now he walked on because there was nothing but death behind him. They were coming for him too, following him across the land.

When Tacoomba reached the end of the earth, there was

another body of endless water. With the war tribe still approaching and tribes in the west still burning, Tacoomba began to swim.

And when he grew tired, out of sight of land, he gave himself up to the water. There he knew the eastern tribe would not burn him.

FIRE-SPEARS

My grandfather's father saw one once. That's how I know it's true.

The wattles were blooming. That's what he remembered. The fresh scent that clung to his breath and poured down his throat, into his lungs. They were plentiful that year, extending farther into unwalked terrain, onto land that was left unsung.

On one of his walks, the kind that takes more than a sun, more than a moon, he looked up. He was lighting his campfire, and the sky people were lighting theirs. He liked to watch their fires and wonder what they did with their day. That's when he saw it.

The weapon flew across the sky; a fire-spear thrown with great power. He knew it was a weapon of the gods, sent to punish one of those sky tribes. He had seen much smaller spears fly before – the short, brief weapons the sky tribes used to fight among themselves.

This fire-spear flew longer than a night. That's how I know he was right. For who could have thrown such a weapon so far if not the gods – The Oort – who live beyond the sky people, past the land of our ancestors?

That's how I know the gods exist.

He never saw which tribe was hit though, or learned their crime that enticed the fire-spear.

GIANT GAME

In the Before, when the nights were dark, men lived in caves, afraid to roam. They knew only their homes and the plains where they hunted.

Blue Feather watched his brothers shoot their arrows straight and throw their spears with precision. They brought much food to the family while Blue Feather only ate.

When the rest of the men planned for the next hunt, Blue Feather crushed grains. Often in the distance he could see the giants playing, shaking and chasming the land with their wrestling. Blue Feather wished he could be like the giants, free to roam and stronger than all of his brothers put together.

A coyote began to join Blue Feather, sitting beside Blue Feather as he completed his tasks.

Eventually, Blue Feather grew comfortable with the coyote, even speaking aloud his wishes and dreams and resentments. Coyote was a good listener.

Then Coyote spoke. "I could help you if you wish. You have moved me with your troubles and no mortal should suffer so."

"What do you want in exchange?"

"Only to help. Though should you dedicate the next hunt to me, that would not go unnoticed."

"But it is Swift Foot who decides who to honor, not me," said Blue Feather.

"The leader offers up, and so I'm asking you."

Blue Feather puffed his chest. He could not resist a glance to Swift Foot, noting his place at the head of the fire. The smoke billowed and Blue Feather could almost mistake his own face in the haze.

HE SAT ON THE TALLEST ROCK AND WAITED.

At first the giants ignored Blue Feather. Then they argued among themselves over who he was watching.

When the giants approached, Blue Feather ignored their questions and when they silenced he offered, "I have a gift for the strongest man among you."

The giants took up his words and all proclaimed that they were the strongest.

Again Blue Feather waited for the giants to quiet. "The only way to decide is with a challenge. Pull up the tree that best fits your hand and string it with a vine. The giant who can shoot his bow the highest is the strongest."

Immediately the giants rushed to make their bows, just as Coyote said they would. Yet as the shooting began there were loud drums in the sky, a bang with each arrow. The giants loved the noise, pulling up all the tiny trees they could find to keep it going.

Blue Feather couldn't decide how to judge who had shot the highest and was therefore the strongest because all of the arrows made the same noise and he could not see where they landed. But this did not matter because the giants soon wandered off to enjoy their game and Blue Feather slipped back to his cave.

When Blue Feather returned, he was celebrated. The hunters had seen him in the distance speaking to the giants and had seen how the giants fled at his words.

Swift Foot exclaimed, "You are braver than I!"

However, when the sun fell the darkness never came. The sky was like a backwards robin's egg, speckled with light. Instead of fearing their caves would crumble from the giants, they now feared the sky would fall.

Swift Foot pressed Blue Feather for details of how he scared off the giants, certain a god had been angered somehow.

As Blue Feather explained, anger rose all around him as the hunters reached for their spears.

He ran as fast as he could, slipping through the few remaining trees, hoping they would protect him.

Coyote joined in, laughing as he darted.

"You said I would lead the hunt!"

"You lead the retreat, so now you can offer up your own death to me," said Coyote, leaving Blue Feather behind in the plains.

SWALLOW

That damn Helioson is such a braggart, always showing off his fire wings. You'd think he was Helios himself, instead of just the first creature to ask for a blessing. He thinks he's such a big-shot. If other gods were giving out blessings, he'd be put in his place right enough.

He's lucky the only other god around isn't even a proper one, but a dead one. And none of the other animals have dared go down into that darkness. But I'm not scared. That Helioson has clipped my wings one time too many, and insulted my flight patterns a thousand times too many.

I dive, pull my wings in like a second ribcage, and give myself over to gravity, to Death.

Not even I am brave enough to look Him in the eye though, so I keep my head low as I'm cushioned by hot air that nearly burns as bad as Helios himself.

"You dare enter my domain?" thunders around me. "Without the grace of giving up breath?"

"My God, please, I humbly beg a blessing," I mumble to the cave floor.

"You swoop in here, uninvited, and dane to speak of requests? You pray for my favor, with nothing given?" rumbles the walls.

"Not a favor. A blessing, a gift. You see," I begin to ramble, "Helios blessed Helioson with wings like fire. He's always showing them off, but the rest of us, we're all the same, all the same except him."

"You wish for Tarturian fires to consume your wings?"

Did I want to have my wings burn up the sky like Helioson? Yes, I wanted what he had, but it would be so much sweeter to possess more; to lord over him as he has us since the blessing.

"Your heart races. You desire more than fire, you crave power." A pause weighs down the darkness. "Very well. Your blessing is granted, go lord it over your peers."

I erupt out of there, glad to be released from such oppressiveness, allow my back to straighten and my wings expand. My chest swells as I gulp in light and air and pride. Helioson isn't the only blessed bird now.

Swooping through the air, I catch each eye I pass. Let them admire my blessing and spread the news. Let Helioson hear and know that he is no longer special.

It doesn't take long before I spot him. I haven't landed yet, prowling the sky, leaving my wings on display.

His double-take gives my wings extra lift, surging past without a glance. I am above him now. The blessed are not required to take notice of others. Until I hear the splash.

The sky empties of color besides boring blue. Beneath me a hulking beast with featherless wings flaps uselessly against the sea.

I soar higher. Now I'm the only blessed bird, the only blessed animal.

It isn't until I perch that I conspicuously examine my blessing. With a glance though I'm knocked to the ground, barely catching my flight with empty wings. What was once ripping blues is now an absence of life. It doesn't make any sense. When Helioson received his blessing, his blue was transformed to a life color, why then is mine not similar?

Helios is sinking, but I don't wait. I shoot past the animals settling in for the darkness and dive back into the cave.

"Returned so soon, my son?" the walls rumble.

"Give it back!"

"I've already given."

"No. No, you've taken. Give me back my color!"

"Did you or did you not come to my cave begging for a blessing? Begging to be set apart from other creatures?" growls the weighted air.

"Well, I..." The air is so heavy, my beak finds the hard dirt.

"You barge into my realm, again, swelled with questions, your feathers ruffled. A blessing requested, a blessing given."

"But I," I turbulence over my words, hardly sorting my thoughts into words before I'm forced to leave his presence, "I ask for another blessing."

"You wish for a blessing?"

"No, no, I request a deal," I rush.

Water trickles deeper within the darkness. "What do you desire?"

"Color."

"Deal." Wind rushes the word against my feathers.

I want to look, to see myself whole again, but there's no light. I'm flown upwards, back among my own kind as Helios matches my rise.

The last vestiges of His voice whispers, "And you'll give your servitude."

"Wait!" But I'm already among the branches and my wings are shadows.

MAUS UPSIDE-DOWN

Maus lived in a meadow, but often he would venture into the woods at night, breathing in the smell of the damp soil and leaves. Crying danger, the other mice warned him away from the forest. Maus thought the other mice were cowards, until one night he was almost caught by Owl. Knowing the dirt well, Maus hid, but learned there was safety in staying at home.

He ignored this wisdom.

Now Owl hated to be outsmarted, and vowed to the night that he would make a meal out of Maus. But Maus was smart too and knew Owl would hunt where Maus lived. Maus would sit below Owl's tree each night before Owl woke up to hunt. Soon Maus started climbing into the trees where Owl would never even think to look for him.

Bats are gossipy creatures and, being fond of drama, had been watching the antics of Maus and Owl. Having been made fun of by Owl for their social practices, the bats hoped Maus would outsmart him.

On the night of a new moon, when Owl could see most clearly, the bats were so overcome with worry for Maus that they clustered around him on the branches, shielding him. Maus sat on the top of the branch while all the bats hung upside down.

This drew more attention to Maus.

The bats told Maus to hang upside down like them and then Owl would never give him a second look, but Maus's feet were too small to grasp even the smallest branch. The bats saw Maus's tail flickering in nervousness and suggested he use his tail to hold onto the branch instead. Maus was very scared that he would fall, but the bats promised to fly down and save him.

Maus spent part of each night learning how to hang from the branches by his tail. Soon a few of the other mice who had also angered Owl fled to the trees and joined Maus and the bats.

After a many moons, Maus and his friends began to forget about their home in the meadows and became so good at swinging by their tails that they thought the other mice were silly not to do it too.

It came to pass that Maus and his friends lived in the trees while the others stayed in the meadows, naming them Opossom and forgetting they were ever family.

HOW WORMS CAME INTO BEING

Many men ago there was a tribe called Sadhu. The Sadhu followed the teachings of Vikrama Ditya, a wise man who had left sacred texts explaining the importance of humility. His texts stated that when meeting an important person, both of his feet must be touched as a sign of respect and admiration. However, the texts were written so long before memory that the Sadhu could not recall how such a rule began and knew only that it was to be obeyed.

Slowly, a sub-sect of the Sadhu began to touch the feet of everyone, to place everyone they met above themselves. Soon a simple touch was not enough and they would sit at a person's feet. Then they began to compete as to who was the most humble among their sect. They each attempted to keep their heads lower than everyone else.

Over time, the entire sect sank themselves closer and closer to the ground until they crawled everywhere for fear of putting their heads above others and being thought too prideful by other members of their sect. Even then they worried about their pride and prayed to the divine for its removal.

One day their bodies began to change. With all of their crawling at the feet of others, their limbs shortened and a smooth slime coated their bodies allowing them to never have to raise their heads from the ground.

When sliding along the dirt, equal with the feet of men, became too prideful, they burrowed underground to be properly humble. And still they live there today beneath the soil, too insignificant to venture to the surface and into the sun.

Maybe the worms have forgotten that they were once Sadhu. Maybe they believe this is the life they deserve. Any who believe differently, who wish for escape from their humble existence, rise to the surface on dark days and are once again equal to the feet of men. There, unwilling to return to their tunnels, they watch the sunrise and bask in the sun's prideful rays.

So far above the rest of their sect, they burn.

HOW THE SMOKING BEGAN

He was passionate while she was cool. This led to many fights that woke their village, but they refused to separate.

When their children moved to homes of their own, the din was like thunder shaking the trees. Even the earth trembled beneath their cries.

When the sun rose again, she walked to the sea. She never walked back into the village.

He sat himself down, right there at the entrance to the village, anger roiling beneath his skin. To pass the time, he puffed on his smokes and watched the sea, trembling still in his rage.

Over time, he grew larger, demanding more space for his righteousness. Forcing the village to move farther inland.

However, the village was glad for the peace and continued on with their lives. It was only occasionally that they would look up at the peak where grandfather now sat and saw the way he smoked in anger.

But the sea would boil right back.

Even after generations, they're still fighting, shaking the ground beneath their feet.

THE WAILS OF DIANA

As a little girl, Diana was afraid of the dark. Her daddy would try a different nightlight each night, but she said the flickering lights made the shadows dance and try to grab at her sheet.

One night in exasperation, instead of plugging in a nightlight, her daddy opened the bedroom curtains and let the moon shine onto Diana's bed.

That night Diana slept peacefully.

Over the years, the moon grew very fond of Diana. So fond that the moon's light never faded or lessened no matter which phase the moon was forced into.

And Diana was just as fond, grateful to the moon for watching over her each night so that she could sleep in peace.

When suitors began to knock at her daddy's door, she turned them away because they did not light her up half so much as her moon. She was so hounded by callers that she slipped into the night under the light of her moon.

Seeking her true love and the suitor she would accept, Diana rushed to the mountains. She climbed higher and higher, gaining on the moon with each step. At the top, when she could go no farther, the moon was huge and luminous, so close she could nearly touch her love.

Some say, Diana stepped back and, with a running start, leaped into the arms of the moon, ready to be caught and united. But she fell short and was caught only by the wind. Her final wail sailed forth through the mountains, echoing to all who listen.

Others say, Diana reached out her hand, but knew she could not touch her love. She was still too far away with no way to gain more height. Having failed in her goal, knowing that she would be forever exiled from her love, Diana broke down and wailed.

She spent her life there on the mountain, as close to her moon as she could get. Grieving and wailing over the distance she could not breach.

THE SISTERS

Andrea holds hands with her sisters. There was no time before and there will be no time after. Together they shift and roll and move. Their edges are buffeted by water as they move slowly away from each other, until only their hands are touching. They were once so close, huddled together against the waves.

Along the ridges of their spines, in the divots of their joints, and across the plains of their bellies, their distant descendants care for the sisters. They walk lightly, vague points of pressure on organs and knots and digits. Their trail of movement stimulating blood flow.

When the sisters are riotous in their motions, their descendants are fearful and whisper soothing prayers to calm them into sleep.

When Andrea wakes she feels lower. She longs to roll and twist with the freedom of her youth, but the descendants are much heavier now, chaining her and her sisters in one position. The water laps higher at her coasts. She is unable to adjust her arms or swing her legs. She tries to stretch, but cannot.

The new points of impact remain still, never moving. They only expand, taking over her body. They do not relieve the pressure or care for the forests of her body, and so she does not thank them with bounty and fuels.

The pressure grows heavier and heavier, pinning her down. When did she become a prisoner?

Andrea gathers all her energy to combat her restraints so the pinions holding her down topple. Her captors, in anger and fear, reattempt constructing her straps. They do not remember the rhythm of the soothing whispers and she forgets kindness. She leads her sisters in revolt against the family that has abandoned them, throwing them off their bodies and releasing the boiling fury from within.

CATHERINE'S WATERFALL

Hikers like the challenge. They come from their cities and their suburbs and stand at the base of the waterfall, thinking to conquer the trail to the cave at the top. They don't listen to the gossip. They ignore the backward locals who dip their hands in the waters to bless their heads. The hikers are here to climb the slippery rocks, to boast to friends at home that they are the only ones to find the source of the water, that they were the first.

THE VILLAGERS STOP OFTEN FOR CATHERINE'S BLESSING and to shake their heads at the sacrilegious foreigners. The elders still claimed to have heard the last echo of Catherine's singing and that their own grandparents remembered the mountains ringing with Catherine's dulcet tones. Those that came before remember the shy little girl who used to sneak up to the highest cave to sing; it could be reached in those days.

And they pass on the story to those who will listen:

Troubles came in the guise of pale faces who tried to steal away the village children and imprison them in their white houses. The villagers fought back. They hid their children in the mountains and prayed to the gods to remove the plague of paleness.

The trouble came closer, searching the area, ever nearer to the hidden children. Catherine, the continual champion of hide and seek, watched the danger approach and led the children higher and higher into her unfindable cave.

When she thought the danger had passed, she left the rest of the children to sneak down to the village to check that it was safe to emerge. But it wasn't safe, for the white men still occupied her village and they beat her for hiding the children. They beat her for not turning the children over to their care and for not speaking their language and for besting their abilities at tracking. They beat her because they could.

But Catherine did not speak. She could not bring herself to form words away from her cave.

As her body hung limp, the men walked away from the village and did not return for many generations. Some said they were ashamed for their actions, some said they were embarrassed for not winning, and some said they were just waiting to make another attack.

Whatever their reasons, the villagers gathered up Catherine's tiny form, cleaning her wounds and wrapping her in the most beautiful shroud that could be found. The children returned and together the village bore Catherine to her cave where she was happiest so the mountains would reverberate with her music.

The villagers often went to her side to weep and give thanks. The children grew up and they cried over their savior. The mourners came for generations. They continue to come. What began as a trickle of tears became a roaring waterfall.

Now instead of the mountains singing with music, they wail with loss.

And still the children of those children come for a blessing.

AND THE PALE FACES HAVE RETURNED, TRYING TO CONQUER her.

THE STAR CHRONICLES

THE STAR CONFLICT

When the stars were young, they fell in love.

Since birth they looked out over the earth, watched humans crawl from the dirt and eventually walk upright. The first humans gave birth to a child, a little boy with round cheeks and tiny fingers. The stars shone brighter with fascination before the boy took his first steps. They rained love down on their human, lighting his way on the darkest nights.

As the boy grew older, he returned the stars' love. He would lie beneath their blanket and bask in their glow. For their amusement he told them stories based on the pictures he found in their faces.

The stars drank in the boy's stories and adoration. They moved in the sky to spread his love equally between them and to provide the boy with more pictures to fuel his stories.

But one star, Nordstern, refused to relinquish his position in the sky. Nordstern claimed that he was best loved by the boy because he featured so heavily in the boy's stories. This antagonized the other stars who began to vie for the boy's affection by burning brighter. Soon the stars were so bright the moon told them to stop or she would extinguish them.

So the stars shone with less light, but a few cheated on the agreement of silence. They began to whisper stories back to the boy through their rays. These returned stories strengthened the boy's love for these particular stars.

Nordstern was among the stars telling the new stories.

Jealousy among the stars grew until war broke out in the sky. Some stars jumped, hoping to escape the fighting and be closer to the boy. Others were pushed, knowing it was death.

The boy died in the light-shower that rained down upon the earth. And his death brought an end to the war among the stars, who vowed from that day forth to never love a human already beloved by one of the brethren.

THE STAR CHRONICLES

THE STAR-LOVERS

The stars' vow lasted for many human generations with each star loving and being loved by their own human. The stars looked away from each others' beloveds; far enough away that no tribe possessed more than one star lover.

Until Nascha, birthed to the plains people.

At Nascha's birth, instead of looking up at her mother, she looked up directly into the rays of Nordstern who looked back. Even though her tribe already belonged to a star, for Nordstern it was love and out of love he told Nascha stories.

As Nascha grew she displayed her wisdom to her tribe. The tribe grew antagonistic. Some tribesman sided with the tribe's shaman, beloved by the star Merope, while others sided with Nascha, the new star lover. There were minor disputes among the tribesman which soon escalated into near war. The tribesmen demanded Nascha give up her star, to respect the stance of the tribe's dominant star lover, but she refused to sever her connection with Nordstern.

When the fighting broke out Nascha watched with heartache as families broke apart and men killed each other for her and her star. When her supporters raised their weapons against the shaman, Nascha tried to stop them, to save the connection of the star and star lover. She stepped between the tribesmen and the shaman as the arrow shot through the air and landed in her heart.

Nordstern shone less bright that night. The tribes cried. The soil where she fell erupted with tears in anguish, for even the earth felt a loss that would never abate.

HOW WHALES CAME INTO BEING

In the beginning there was sea and sky. The world was made in shades of blue. Everything, that is, except for Helioson with his flashy red and yellow feathers tipped in orange. He said he was blessed and made in the sun's image while the rest of them were made by someone else, someone less important. This offended the other animals, who resented Helioson's colorful plumage.

Then, one day, Helioson saw a new bird with wing tips of the palest blue, so light in fact that he wondered if they were almost a new color. They were not nearly as brilliant as himself of course, but he did not like this change and did not like to think that other animals too would have color. Only he was the colorful one, the special one.

So on this day, Helioson flew high over this other bird to glint so wonderfully in the sun, to let them know he was the sun's own bird and to remind them that they were nothing. But Helioson flew too high, blinded by the glare from their pale wing tips.

The sun was offended at his lack of respect in coming so near. As punishment, the sun burned Helioson's brilliant plumage and threw him down into the ocean. There, Helioson turned blue and heavy.

Now Helioson was the same color as everyone else and blended into the water he so detested. He tried to jump back into the air but was too heavy and fell continuously back into the sea.

And still to this day he prays the sun will forgive him and give him back his beauty. But the sun hasn't and Helioson jumps to the sky only to fall. He says until he is beautiful again he cannot be called Helioson because that is a name for a blessed bird.

Until then, he calls himself Whale.

POSEIDON'S BRIDE

CHELSEA

The tide is still up, along with the moon and the last few stars. We gather in our pale blue shifts, shivering slightly in the morning cold, a flock of hopefuls to witness the ceremony. Even the matrons wear blue, but of a darker shade, more reminiscent of the hidden depths than the shallow cove.

As the tide turns, Chelsea steps forward, her pristine white slip glowing, a delicate wreath of seaweed balancing around her crown. We watch with bated breath as first her toes and then her calves are swallowed by the sea. The tide pulls her deeper out to our lord, covering her hips and breasts. Chelsea never looks back, focused on her potential husband's home; her home.

The wave comes as it always does, devouring Chelsea and sweeping her down to the depths of our lord. Our eyes do not waver. We wait for the sign of acceptance.

But we receive instead the rejection. Chelsea's carefully woven crown washes up onto the beach with an insignificant wave. We stare at the tiny circle lying peacefully on the smoothed brown sand.

No one touches it.

As the last stars wink out, we slip away from the beach, our arms linked. We murmur quietly among ourselves. Marianne is next, turning sixteen at the end of the week. Will she be accepted? Will her crown of seaweed become a crown of coral? Will our lord accept her as his wife?

If Marianne's crown washes ashore, there will still be a chance for us. Our own opportunity to be accepted by Poseidon awaits.

POSEIDON'S BRIDE

MARI

Waking up, Mari is not prepared to open her eyes. Not yet. Clinging to sleep and dreams, the smooth touch of silk clashes with memories of the dewy tickle of grass. Stretching her limbs, the feather soft bed gives beneath her and the blanket slips, exposing her skin and night-slip to the cool breeze flowing over the bed.

The breeze brings in the smell of salt, assaulting her nostrils, burning away the memory of wildflowers and dirt that was so prominent in the dream's meadow. The harsh brine forces her to open her eyes to examine these differences closer.

Her vision is filled with red embroidered silk, yellow gladioli in a red field. Unable to resist, she brushes her fingers along their threaded petals as they drift into the pillow's fringe. Through the fringe, she continues into the valley and up over the next meadow of pillow.

Atop this red meadow, her fingertips encounter a crinkly slip of paper. Gripping the edge lightly, Mari rolls onto her back, bringing the small paper with her until she holds it directly overhead, the yellow of time creeping from the edges towards her name, written in beautiful calligraphy at the very center. Flipping the note over Mari reads, in the same script:

όταν είσαι έτοιμος

When you're ready.

Mari drops the note to her chest and stares up at the imitation sky, watching the stars fade as the morning light creeps farther into the room.

Ready for what?

Throwing off the blankets, she sits up to take in the room properly. The walls are made of sheer curtains, billowing in the breeze creating an undulating effect like waves. The only other piece of furniture in the room is a delicate vanity made from what appears to be coral.

Curiously, on the little stand before the mirror there sits less of a box and more of a large clam, gleaming. Unable to resist, Mari crosses the room to pick it up, feeling the solid weight, wondering what is inside. She opens the clam and admires a tiara resting within; a small froth of pearls. Gently stroking each individual pearl, she watches as the dewdrops soak in her affection and gleam brighter for the love.

A soft splash pulls Mari's gaze to the insubstantial walls. Outside is not the meadow of her childhood, nor of her dream, but an endless expanse of shimmering blue thrown out before her, reaching out into the horizon. At her feet the marble floor drops to steps disappearing into the shallows.

Sitting upon the edge she clutches the note in her hands as she dips her feet in the salt water and contemplates how she came to be adrift in this blue meadow.

The glare of the sun off the mirror surface of the water causes Mari to squint, but she continues to search the horizon. Searching for any sign to tell her what she should do now.

Anything besides the note left by the bed.

Two dolphins glide, unafraid, up to the steps. They loll onto their sides to stare up at Mari. She reads the question in their eyes, will she follow them into the depths?

When she shakes her head, denying them, they swim away, turning often to look back to where Mari sits atop the steps.

Yesterday she was hiding in the meadow from her father. She remembers lying among the tall grasses watching the clouds drift past, heading for places far in the wind. A young man with a halo of hair and blue eyes, deeper than the creek she bathed in. There was a tiny shell too, nestled in the hollow of his throat, bright against his sun-kissed skin.

He gave an outstretched hand, rough with callouses, and asked, "Will you walk with me?"

She can't recall the details, but how she misses those eyes, his touch, already, even more than her grass meadow full of wildflowers and dirt.

Running her fingertips across the script yet again, she admires the elegant loops and controlled lines of ink. The dolphins are still watching from the horizon when she pushes to her feet and returns to the coral vanity, her feet marring the bare floor with wet prints becoming salty outlines.

Mari props the note against the mirror and settles the pearl tiara among the nest of her curls. A look of resignation enters her green eyes. She doesn't linger on her reflection, walking back through the foaming white curtains. She hesitates infinitesimally before lowering her first foot back into the sea. Step by step she walks into the depths, head held at a regal height, a becoming position for such a tiara.

The dolphins watch her progress from a distance. The water rises up her thighs, over her hips, up to her shoulders. At the next step the water flows through the tiara's pearls, but they hold to her crown, unwilling to be separated from Mari.

Mari walks into the ocean's depths. The dolphins swim down to meet her and lead the way.

HOW FILBERT CONTORTED

I had a name once, of that I'm fairly sure. Every mother names their boy, and I'm here so it stands to reason I must have had a mother at some point. A father too, but I don't remember either of them. I've been called many things in my travels, but they're not my name.

The Romans called me Avellano when I walked through their cities, tracking soldiers from the battlefield. Troy was a long way from there. My body grew old before I crossed into the north, unable to move into the underworld. She won't let me. This is my punishment.

The Irish, for now they were named this, called me Filbert. But again this is not my true name. Athena took this too as punishment, along with my mortality. All she left me with was my ability to age, and my contorting limbs.

I learned my lesson halfway across the continent, to never sleep. That is when my gifted helmet was stolen and that is what I seek. Once I can offer it back in homage of my goddess, maybe then she will let me sleep. Let me cross the river with Charon, though most around me have forgotten his name. Just as I have forgotten my own.

So now I'm Filbert as I step slowly across the green fields, slowing down, creaking.

Until my limbs refuse to move, too contorted to carry on in my search.

Stuck, I wait for the goddess to forgive, but she's too used to war. Stuck, I watch as a boy plays in the field across from me. He laughs as he holds up a shiny helmet, surprised at his find. If I were able, I'd weep as he carries it home to show his family.

If I hadn't dawdled so in my youth, maybe now I wouldn't be this, a Contorted Filbert in a foreign field.

TONGUES

There came a day the tower fell and let forth a cascade of tears and tongues.

Generations built the tower, brick by brick and word by word. Each belonged to everyone, but afterward each was alone. They were a community of song until they sat among the cracked stones and gave voice to individual wails that belonged to no one, barely even to the wailers themselves.

A few tried to rebuild, but their words and bricks no longer fit.

Soon they wandered off into deserts and fields, each to their own. They walked away from the people they no longer understood, searching for a new home and a new commonality.

When they met others they would try to share a moment, a thought or two, but their words fell on uncomprehending ears. So they wandered away again, putting ever more distance between themselves and the tower and tongue that once unified them.

A few rare people eventually came across another who

shared their new tongue. This was a cause for more tears, this time in joy, and they would gather, settling in the place of their meeting or wandering on together.

But many more individuals have not found another with whom they can speak. Some continue their search across new environments. Still others have given up hope, settling in silence or with another individual they cannot understand.

THE PREACHER

The crowd jostles Peter as he makes his way over to the tree. He clutches a small stool to his chest, careful not to impale any of his tormentors.

When he arrives at the tree there is a fresh carving on the trunk, 'Judas'. Peter wants to run his hand over the word, to wash the tree's flesh clean, but refuses to give the watching crowd the satisfaction. Instead Peter settles the stool into the grooves made the day before and the day before that, all the way back to his conversion twenty years ago.

Slowly Peter reaches into his bag and pulls out his good book. It's worn from days of preaching, like his spine and knees, but the three together keep him upright in some form. He continues on with the hope of betterment for the masses, given through his reading, through his words and daily discovery of new understanding.

He steps one foot at a time onto the stool, adjusts his feet. They'll be sore soon, but Peter knows he is following the righteous path. He opens his book and begins reading from the beginning. He always skips his conversion story as he is but a small unimportant messenger for the greater good. He starts at the beginning with the magic of creation out of nothing.

"Before there was something, there was nothing, a singularity which inflated over billions of years..."

He doesn't look up as he reads, his good book holds him rapt, but not the crowd streaming by, a river of uncaught fish. He doesn't see as they swim closer, creating an island of his stool, creating a whirlpool spiraling inward. Peter only pauses at the collision as the crowd swallows him before coughing him up with a twisted yoke, a lead thrown over a branch.

They pull him upright, crying, "Judas!"

Peter doesn't resist, but wishes for the comfort of his good book, lost in the chaos. He knows his own death dance will be nothing compared to the neutron stars. He hangs from his tree where he stood for so many years educating the masses who refused his teachings until the university collects his willed body for study.

GLEIPNIR AND THE HUMANS

The first race after the gods retreated to their mountain was a warrior race led fearlessly into battle by bow-women. They could shoot arrows to wind through the forest, catching prey and foe alike. Only those who proved themselves in battle could lead their tribes and the stronger warriors had the best choice when taking a man to husband, if they even chose to bestow that honor.

No warrior would take Thurmon to husband as he was not useful in the home. He could not keep a fire lit nor was he docile in conversation. He was forever distracted and interrupting. Thurmon's family was embarrassed by his remaining at home for so many years, past the age when most boys were welcomed into the homes of their wives. Even his father was ashamed for though he doted on his son, he knew Thurmon would not be courted by a worthy warrior.

Thurmon did not listen to the advice of his family. He would sit and watch from the hilltop as the hunters stalked from their valley village to the surrounding woods. Each morning he would rise before the sun to watch Ylva lead her band of warriors out for the kill. He loved to watch her long legs as she ran and the graceful way she drew a bow. She was daughter to Hertha who led the village. The other boys laughed at useless Thurmon for dreaming so high, saying that Ylva would never look his way, but would take someone helpful for a husband.

But Thurmon was not dissuaded in his affection, though Ylva never once spoke to him.

Only when the rumors began in the marketplace did Thurmon begin to grow anxious. The entire village was abuzz about Ylva considering taking a husband. Everyone tried to imagine the contenders, dreaming who could be a worthy consort to such a powerful warrior.

Thurmon wanted so badly to be chosen. In desperation he decided, instead of watching Ylva begin her hunt from the vantage point of the hill, he would situate himself in his finest vest and trousers directly outside the fort where her mother ruled. This way she would be sure to see him at his best and she would immediately ask for his hand in marriage.

Yet that morning, as Ylva left her home, her eyes slid right over Thurmon and she didn't stop to compliment him on his fine clothes or on the new way he had brushed his hair. Watching Ylva take off for the woods, Thurmon could not prevent his face from flushing. All this time he had dreamed that if she only noticed him, she would fall instantly in love. He had dreamed of soothing her aches after battles and telling her stories to keep her happy.

Again the next day, Thurmon made the same attempt, but this time he was more forward, despite his father's advice that women do not want such a trait in their husbands. As soon as Ylva appeared in her doorway, Thurmon stepped towards her and asked, "Ylva, may I walk with you to the hunt today?"

Ylva looked squarely at Thurmon and squinted her eyes. "Who are you? Why are you keeping me from my hunt?"

"Sorry, Ylva," he said, trying to hide his impatience and act like a proper man. "I am Thurmon, son of Kira. I was hoping to have a moment of your company today. May I walk with you?"

"Neither the woods nor the hunt are a place for men. Go home to your family or I shall have to have a word with your mother about your inappropriate conduct," said Ylva as she walked away, leaving Thurmon standing by the side of the road.

Even worse than being dismissed by the warrior he loved, many villagers were in the area and saw his embarrassment. Again Thurmon's face reddened. He wanted to show Ylva that he was a worthy match for her; if she wouldn't love him, he would make her. He just had to figure out how - how to make a strong warrior his wife. The townspeople wouldn't laugh at him then.

Thurmon walked through the outskirts of the village, avoiding the gossip of his failure. His wandering brought him closer to the woods than he would have liked, but this was the only place he could find peace. No one besides the women ever came anywhere near the woods.

When Thurmon heard the voices of a few of the boys he had been to school with, he scrambled to the edge of the woods to hide in the shrubbery. He would take the terrors of the wood over the relentless teasing of his newlywed peers. As the voices crept closer, he ducked farther into the trees so as not to be seen as the group passed.

It was at this moment that Thurmon stumbled backwards upon a cleared, sunlit path through the trees. Having never seen this track from the outside, Thurmon gathered all his courage to walk deeper into the wood. If he was brave, maybe he would stand out enough for Ylva to choose him as her consort.

The path was quite wide, wide enough for a cart, but

Thurmon could not see the way out of the woods from where he stood. Deeper into the woods, the path grew gradually steeper in small amounts, but was never tough to climb.

Ringing steel called Thurmon to a large bright clearing which embraced a tiny cabin. He hesitated at the edge of the path. While he had been almost comfortable walking through the woods, the idea of approaching these unseen warriors left him weak and terrified. The moment these women saw him, they would send him directly home and tell his mother of his disobedience. Edging along the trees, trying to shield himself, he crept closer to see if one of the warriors was his beloved Ylva.

He nearly fainted when he had finally snuck around the clearing. The two warriors, clanging swords and hardly sweating with the effort, were men.

For as long back as Thurmon could remember, men had never been allowed anywhere near swords; they were considered far too dangerous for boys. Yet here were two men fighting just as well as any woman warrior he had ever seen.

Inching closer, Thurmon inadvertently kicked a rock, causing the two men to drop their swords and look in his direction. Without the rapid movement, the men appeared like stone, massive and pale; one with hair like the midnight sky and the other like sunshine. They stared at Thurmon as Thurmon stared at them.

"This is not your place, boy," called the man with the sunshine hair. "You should turn back. Return to your people."

Thurmon was too scared to move, let alone give a proper response. So he remained standing at the edge of the clearing, taking in the sight of these two awe inspiring swordsmen.

"If you have something to say child, out with it," said the midnight haired man. He twirled his sword nonchalantly as he spoke, like a young girl with a stick.

"How is it you are allowed to work with the weapons of women?" asked Thurmon.

"Ah, you have a fascination with steel," said the dark haired one, tossing his weapon from hand to hand. "It was always ours until your women stole the methods."

Watching the steel arc through the air, and the men holding these dangerous threats so fearlessly, Thurmon was entranced enough to step free of the trees and into the clearing.

"The one I love, Ylva, is a strong warrior, but even she cannot swing with your strength."

"And what of yours?" asked the sunlit man, turning his gaze full on Thurmon, and drawing Thurmon farther into the clearing.

"Women fight, men are supposed to take care of the home. I am not strong enough to hold a weapon," said Thurmon, distracted by the glint of the steel, unwilling to admit to the problem of his heart before two men as strong as women.

"Go home boy. We do not interfere in the lives of the First Race," said the man with sunlight hair, walking away and into the tiny cabin. He didn't close the door though, instead propping it open with a hammer.

Both Thurmon and the midnight haired man watched the sunlit man leave. "He knows I will not now be able to close the door," the dark swordsman grumbles before leaning in towards Thurmon. "Forget my brother. I will solve your problem."

"Umm..." Thurmon shifted his weight from foot to foot.

"Come tell me what you truly desire," said the man with a glinting eye.

Without thought Thurmon said, "To be Ylva's consort."

With a wink the man reached into his breast pocket and pulled out a short, nearly transparent thread. "This is Gleipnir. Tie the ends together and slip it on the finger of your beloved and she will be yours forever."

Thurmon held out his hand so the man could pool the air-light chain in his palm, which warmed to the feather weight. "Thank you."

"Now go on home before my brother gets back, he wouldn't like to know I've made this gift to one of his namesakes." One more wink and the dark haired swordsman entered the cabin, leaving Thurmon standing alone in the clearing.

Slowly, Thurmon walked back into the woods and down the path to the village. When he arrived it was nearly dark, but he went to the market to seek out Ylva, who by now would have returned to distribute the spoils of the hunt. Standing at the edge of the marketplace, Thurmon spotted Ylva's shining red hair through the crowd. Keeping an eye on her, he quickly tied the two ends of the string together as instructed and rushed over to her side.

"Ylva," said Thurmon.

"How many pieces do you require?" asked Ylva, not looking up.

"Ylva, we spoke earlier. I am Thurmon. May I walk with you this evening?"

Glancing briefly at Thurmon's face, Ylva scrunched her eyes, trying to remember him. "Did I not tell you that you should be home? It's getting late. Your father will be expecting you to help with the cooking."

"Yes, he sent me to fetch the meat." Accepting a packet of deer, Thurmon quickly slid the ring of thread on Ylva's finger. "May I please escort you home after market?"

Thurmon met Ylva eye to eye, as she looked up, startled. He counted four blinks of her sharp green eyes.

"I would like that very much. Thank you." There was even a blush in her freckled cheeks.

That night Thurmon walked Ylva back to her home, bursting with joy as she fiddled nervously with her hands like a little school boy. In the morning, he again escorted Ylva to and from the forest, carrying her bow and arrows for her. Eventually, she taught him to string the bow and loose the arrows himself. He even convinced her to let him join the hunt, even though the other hunters did not want a man in their ranks.

When Thurmon and Ylva married, they were the only couple where the woman acquiesced to all the wishes of the man. There was outrage among the women, but the men who originally taunted Thurmon seethed with jealousy. Only much later, when Thurmon ruled the village alone did he finally share his secret with a few other males. He told them of the cabin and the woods and Gleipnir, which, lashed round the finger of his bride, made her completely obedient.

Soon the other men grew brave enough to saunter off and request their own piece of Gleipnir from the black-haired swordsman in the woods; to chain a ring onto the finger of their own wives.

LILLIAN

The raspberries were wet and slippery on their bushes. Between brambles, Lillian dried her fingers on her apron. Bearing her basket farther along the path, she wondered, does Mother actually expect me to fill such a large basket?

The raspberries were wetter the farther she ventured into the woods. Her basket grew heavier with each passing bush. Only when her basket brimmed did she note the glen where the path halted, her pretty little shoes squelching through the grass. The sun shone more brightly there with no trees to steal the warmth. Surely, she thought, I could rest my weary body before I must carry the gathered raspberries home.

The grass was cool as it tickled the back of her neck, gainsaying the heat upon her face. Yes, later, later the long path home would still remain. Lillian soon drifted on the wind of dreams, a smile blossoming on her countenance.

Lillian's skin radiated heat, the sun high overhead as she woke. Combing her fingers through the grass, she stretched to revive her mind and body from such heavenly slumber. Sitting up, surprise rippled through her heart at the young man lounging beside her dropping raspberries into his mouth. Blithe was his face, with full lips and heavy eyes. His limbs were clad in green satin, difficult to see against the grass. Embroidered silver fish leaped about his cuffs, brighter than a full moon. Resting upon his breast lay a single clover, wrought of water to ripple with the breeze.

Her eyes widened at the swimming fish, unaccustomed to living embroidery.

"Good Sir, why do you eat all my berries?" Lillian asked.

"Good morning, little girl. You've slept quite late and I grew hungry watching you dream so," he replied, his words punctuated with red dropping from fingertips to lips.

"That's all well and good, sir, but now I must return with my basket only half full, for the bushes are now bare."

"Exactly why I waited for you. Come, I will show you the most delicious raspberries. I know all the best hiding places."

"I'm not certain I should. Mother waits for me. I should return to the village."

"Do not worry, little girl. These bushes are not far. Only a dozen steps more and a few trees and there we'll be. 'Tis better to return home to your mother with a full basket as she asked. These raspberries are much better than any you've found yet in your valley," he said, nimbly rising, her basket in tow.

Lillian scrambled to her feet, nearly stumbling on her apron, streaked brown and red from gathering. Following him deeper into the forest, she saw the man balancing on an overturned trunk. He was whistling a tune, bright and fair, as he swung the basket to and fro.

"Come little girl. The day is long, but the sun is already at his peak," he said, vaulting from the log to the ground, leaving Lillian to struggle over on her own.

"That is not my name. I am not Little Girl. I will be ten

years old next month and my name is Lillian," she said, hands fisted on hips because he was not being nice.

At this, the man stopped his hurried steps and bowed with so many flourishes, a blush rose in her cheeks. "And I am no sir. You may call me Cainnech, for that be my name in your tongue. Come, taste these, the sweetest berries to crunch between your teeth," he said, righting himself and gesturing to the west.

And there, beside a pond lay rows of bushes drooping with the weight of so many lush raspberries. The berries smelled tantalizing, drawing Lillian closer. Passing Cainnech she found the basket returned to her hands and had soon plucked red bulbs from the bushes until the basket again overflowed. The last berry circumvented the basket and dropped directly into her own mouth; the tiny seeds crunched, juice dribbled, hands sticky. Truly, Cainnech spoke true.

"Come, Little Lily, clean your face in this chilled pond. Throw off your slippers and dance about in the shallow waters." Cainnech crashed through the surface until he reached one of several large rocks impeding the monotony of the landscape. There he danced with an imaginary figure in circles, his image reflected below, and continued his whistling tune.

Few children danced in the village and music was discouraged. Such a curiosity he was; Mother would never approve.

Lillian shed her own slippers much slower and eased her toes into the brisk waters, holding up the hem of her skirt. Mother would take a switch to her should she return home with mud on her dress. She washed her face quickly and mimicked Cainnech's dancing. Some day a man shall dance with me in such fashion, she thought, content to dream white dresses betwixt orange flowers.

The air cooled as the sun began to hide behind the treetops. Lillian stopped dancing, the peace replaced with fear. She splashed out of the water and slipped into her slippers, no longer minding the hem.

"I really must be going now for Mother is waiting. Thank you Cainnech for showing me these wonderful berries."

As she reached the edge of the trees, her manners returned; she pivoted to throw a quick curtsy in Cainnech's direction where he still stood atop the small rock island, big enough only for him.

———

WHEN NEXT MOTHER SENT LILLIAN OUT TO THE WOODS, now for mushrooms, she could not help but take tiny steps and look about often to catch if she was being watched from the shadows; only crows met her eyes, perched upon branches along the trail. Without consent her feet carried her forward, back to the glen, back to the pond, curious if she would again meet the funny man calling himself Cainnech.

Stepping onto the soaked bank, her heart lowered deeper into her chest, dismayed to find no satin clad body reposed upon a grassy bed. Lillian wanted to search for him along the entire bank, but disallowed this, fearing that he did not wish to be sought. Instead she contented herself with searching beneath nearby trees and shrubbery for mushrooms to fill her basket, hoping that each time she bent back a low slung branch she would discover not a fungus, but his round laughing face.

Oddly, these self same bushes that were only a week ago laden with raspberries now shielded an abundance of fat, squat little mushrooms that Lillian could not recall seeing there before.

Only once her basket was well laden was there a soft, gay whistle giving life to the first few bars of a jaunty tune. Turning, she spied a lithe green figure settled upon the barren rock amid the still water, hands in lap, with his head tilted, attentive to her presence.

Lillian called out as he seemed disinclined to venture forth, "Well met, good Cainnech."

Abruptly silencing the ditty between notes, he rose and pranced from rock to rock to embankment. He dropped into a deep bow and said, "Good day, Little Lily. Well met. You have returned to my pond."

Again tilting his head, he examined her face as if he could not comprehend the creature which stood before him.

"I'm searching the woods for mushrooms and followed the trail here to your very shores. Heavy now sits my bounty in this small basket I carry."

"Over taxed you are for such a little thing. Come, let us rest here upon the grass for these clouds make such funny animals in the sky." With this declaration he walked to a patch of grass lavishly boarded with lush flowers.

Sitting amid the beauty, Lillian's heart slowed, languishing her movements. Indeed unnoticed before, there was a small, colorful field opposite the embankment where an abundance of flowers grew entwined, uncaring of boundaries: Statice, Aster, Gladiolus, Globe Amaranth, and Queen Anne's Lace. Nestled opposite, Cainnech's hands made haste, neatly plucking these last flowers and fashioning them into a crown to settle upon her brow.

"They are a beautiful gift. Thank you."

In turn they lay back against the giving ground, searching the clouds for tales and images. His stories were so lifelike, bringing the clouds to sharper sight. This was much nicer than hurrying home to more chores and Mother; so pleasant to have a friend.

The woods were dark and a little terrifying with the noises of so many strange animals and their bright eyes piercing the leafy walls. Only when Lillian reached the glen could she make out the moon shining bright and full, lighting her steps until the pond spread out before her feet. She wrapped her cloak tighter and perched on a low rock along the bank, admiring the moon shimmer upon the still water.

A rustle caused her to turn, looking towards the woods in search of the cause. Only when she turned back to the lake was he poised on the flat rock island. Nimbly he leaped to smaller rocks only barely peaking above the waterline, until he landed at her feet and fell into a flawless bow.

"Good evening, my little Lily," he said and stooping down, cupped her hands in his. "How fairs your day and now your night?"

"Spent. Aye, we have washed and spun the wool from shearing. Mother says this year's cloth shall be white and I fear she plans too much for my future. But glad I am to say that I sit now here beside you, Cainnech."

"My little Lily, glad is my heart to clasp your hand 'twixt mine."

"Nay, I am not so wee a girl now."

"Aye, tis true. Your brow matches now my lips." Cainnech brushed a kiss across her forehead. "You are a woman grown, no longer the wee child who played on my shores."

"Yet still you are unchanged, not a day have you aged while the years fall behind me."

"These are not the words to whisper beneath such a lively moon. Come, let us dance beneath these stars, throwing light and guidance for our feet."

With such a proclamation, Cainnech rose and pulled Lillian upright, directly into his arms. He held her tight, swinging her fast and sweeping her off her feet. She clung tighter, pleased for an excuse to clasp his firm shoulders.

Lillian's heart was all a-flutter as he set her back on the ground, one arm strong around her waist, the other lightly supporting her right hand. She allowed herself to rest her free hand at his nape, where his hair feathered against his neck, so soft and fine. Lillian responded to his every movement, stepping and swirling and swaying.

The moon was high before they paused to draw breath.

"Our time draws short and I must return to the valley and my bed ere Mother wakes and finds me gone."

"It is sorry indeed the raspberries are long devoured and the ground grows hard with winter, preventing our company beneath the sun, leaving us only the moon."

"The day may be theirs, but the night is ours. Cainnech, farewell until next we meet." She caressed the clover pinned where his heart beat slow. She let his hand slip from hers as he stepped to the water's edge.

When Lillian reached the treeline, she turned for one last farewell. Cainnech stood tall and regal atop his rock, a lone shadow in a black pond.

BRANCHES AND THORNS TORE AT LILLIAN'S DRESS AND VEIL as she ran through the woods, unable to follow the path hidden beneath the fresh snowfall. Tears froze on her cheeks before she could wipe them away. Her entire body shivered with cold and heartache; no cloak to warm her body, no say over her fate.

Glad she was to be again out of doors. She could not count the days since last she had breathed fresh air. Since her mother turned the key on her door and pronounced her betrothed. If only she could have spoken with Cainnech. He would have saved her. But no, she found no way to escape her entrapment.

Standing outside the church, waiting to be led down the aisle, even then, Lillian had not been able to hide the tears. She'd stood at one end, young, prisoner and in love with another; he'd stood at the other, aged, jailor and a mandate.

Mother had tried to force a fatal sentence on her, though Lillian vowed her heart lay elsewhere. Unable to take a single step towards that matrimonial affair, she ran. Even Mother could not stand beside her for the entirety of the day. She ran to the only place Mother would not follow; to the dark woods, home of legends and Lillian's future.

The pristine white of her dress camouflaged her against the snow and she heard no steps, only the baying of the dogs giving chase. Crossing the glen, Lillian slowed her steps, faltering only a little under the weight of the fabric. When she reached the pond, the rock lay barren for Cainnech was not there, nor should be she.

Lillian could not stand there and wait, for then she would freeze or, worse, a hound's jaw may come upon her to force her hand. Oh, where shall I go, she thought, scanning the forest in hopes of a sign. Continually, her eyes drew back to Cainnech's rock, hoping he would hear her heart crying out to his.

But alas, he came not.

Aye, if he would not come to her, then Lillian must go to him; a bride beseeching sanctuary, a woman pleading for love.

Lillian gathered her dress and balanced from stepping stone to stepping stone until she stood alone on the island rock, just wide enough to encompass her white dress. How different the trees looked from here. How distant the shore. She could hardly hear the birds though she knew their calls so well.

Straightening her dress and arranging her veil, for she wanted to look her best for the journey, Lillian gathered her courage and jumped.

HEAVY IS MY HEART AS I CLIMB TO MY ROCK, THE BRIDGE between my home and hers. Today was her wedding day. The crows have laughed at my predicament, my heart's desire bound for eternity to another. Unwilling to gaze upon the sun on such a bleak day, I've hidden below in my own realm. Already her absence weighs on my limbs. My feet are not so nimble for they are not dancing to her. Centuries now I've danced alone upon these shores, but how short the time adored.

What's this, bumping against my rock? A cloud floats upon my pond, usually so barren. Such soft beauty draws my steps, looking a pleasant place to rest.

But no! That face encapsulated there, it cannot be! My veiled love stares unseeing back at me. How lovely she appears and this must be her dreaded gown, now a shroud. A single tear, the first I've formed, drops to kiss her frozen lips, a blemish I must surely dissipate. I lean in to brush them dry with mine own and rectify her piety. With this single touch, the cloud, my shrouded love, slips from the surface replaced by my own reflection.

Those eyes once so familiar now lackluster, though still not a wrinkle has taken hold. Slowly the image is replaced; a single green leaf, a duplicate of the very pendant guarding my heart rises from the shadowy bottom to unfurl in sleep upon the silent pond. And there resting in its heart lies a single white flower, delicate as a cloud.

A water lily.

LOVELESS LEGEND OF THE MAINZ PARROTS

Green parrots were brought from deep Africa to the Rhine Valley to be studied at the university. The cages sat on tables scattered around a white room.

One day a young scientist left a window open and, as he was refreshing the water in the cages, five birds escaped, flying right over his head.

The five green parrots settled into a nearby tree to acclimatize to their return outdoors and the colder temperature of the area. Four of the birds wanted to start flying south to their home, but the fifth bird refused. His mate was still caged in the white room and he did not want to leave her.

The parrots could feel the autumn setting in around them and begged the fifth parrot to fly with them. Still, he refused. The other birds did not want to leave him to die in the cold alone and agreed to stay. The birds' feathers fluffed as winter arrived and they sheltered in pine trees along the river; never straying too far from the green parrots in the white room.

Many times they flew back to the window, clawing at the glass, to rescue the lost love, to view the faces of their caged comrades, but each attempt was met with failure. Every winter the four parrots repeated the routine of asking the fifth to fly south with them, home, and he refused.

Eventually, four of the parrots mated and populated the area along the river as the fifth parrot continued to mourn his love. One by one the original parrots succumbed to old age until only the parrots born along the river remained. They knew nothing but stories of a place that didn't exist. They did not know that they could leave, or the way to do so, or how to find their brethren in another home.

Thus, green parrots came to populate the Rhine Valley.

LEAGUE OF CASANOVAS

PART ONE

The spring air slips in through the bottom of the open window as I trail dreamily up the stairs and into a bubble bath. Careful to keep my hair out of the tub, I cannot help but recall the warmth of Mr. Spencer's body.

I was sitting in the sun at one of those the sidewalk tables of the cafe just down the road. I was sipping rose tea at the time, when this small, lanky man walked over to block my sun and simply said, "Hi, I'm Mr. Mark Spencer and I would like to get to know you. May I join you for a cup of tea?"

He was so sweet in his blue button down and jeans, with kind eyes and patient questions. More than a handful of similar such dates and he keeps getting better and better.

We were on a midnight picnic to watch the stars. He thought of everything for my comfort: extra blankets, a carafe of hot tea, and sweets to keep us awake. He mixed stories of his childhood with those of the ancient gods who now decorate the night sky. I learned a lot that night, both academic and personal. Not once through the long hours we've spent together though has he crossed the line and been less than gentlemanly. Always considerate, polite, almost chaste in his adoration.

Refreshed, I stand and allow the bath water to slide from my body as I admire my shape in the venetian looking glass. Pleased with my figure, I pat myself dry with one of the fluffy white towels stacked on a shelf in the corner. Allowing the air to reach every inch of me, I sit myself before the looking glass to apply minimal makeup; a hint of rogue in my cheeks, a slight shade atop my eyelids, a touch of blush on my lips. I want to look my best for Mr. Spencer.

Counting out one hundred brush strokes, I dream of Mr. Spencer's image superimposed on my own. His cocoa eyes sharp over my baby blue irises. His long Roman nose over my button nose. His thin serious lips over my plump mouth. Only when my hair shines do I set down my brush and walk over to my cupboard to find the perfect dress. My fingertips graze the row of hangers, halting on a silk day dress. It wraps around my hourglass shape, making me feel like Venus amid the sea foam.

The doorbell rings and I float down the stairs, anxious to again be in the company of such a wonderful man. When I open the door, there with nothing but air between Mr. Spencer and I, I struggle to restrain myself from stepping into his arms, but I need to be all that is proper.

"Good evening, Miss Fields," says Mr. Spencer, taking hold of my hand and kissing it.

A blush spreads additional color and warmth through my body.

"Good evening, Mr. Spencer," I say, drawing back my hand. "Please, won't you come in."

I lead him into the parlor to a hand-painted table laden with fresh scones, cold cream and hot tea.

"Well this looks mighty fine," says Mr. Spencer pleasantly.

"You're very kind," I say, pouring the tea for us both.

"It's not every day a beautiful woman invites me to tea. I want to make the experience as pleasant as possible so as to be invited back again in the future."

"Already enticing me into issuing a second invitation?"

"I'll accept any offer you wish to issue."

To such a scandalous remark I only smile and sip my tea, my demure stance negating any forwardness read into my previous comment.

Stepping back from the edge of such an unseemly conversation, Mr. Spencer slips into light chatter; the weather, the furnishings, tidbits of nothingness that make up one's day.

When the teapot is empty, I carefully settle my teacup on its saucer and smile. "Would you like a small tour?"

"I would be honored," says Mr. Spencer, rising from his chair.

He walks over to my own chair and pulls it out from the table for me to stand before presenting me with his elbow. I settle my hand into the crook of his arm, feeling his pulse beat almost erratic through his veins. I escort him through the rooms, calling his attention to paintings by great masters and vases from long ended dynasties.

When we enter the library my own pulse scatters in anticipation. "This is my favorite room in the house."

"It is a well-proportioned room," says Mr. Spencer, scanning the space which is broken up with cozy reading nooks and pillars.

Unhooking myself from Mr. Spencer I stroll along the center promenade of the room until I reach the last pillar. I lean against it, hiding it from view as I direct his attention elsewhere.

"Have you noted the books?" I ask, nodding toward the walls filled with ancient tomes as I caress the pillar.

"Have you read many of them?"

"A few, but I think they look nice and lend an air sophistication to the room."

"They do a wonderful job of it," he says with a smile. "It is late, I should be leaving. I don't want to monopolize your day."

"I'll show you to the door," I say, giving one last hug to the pillar.

I walk back over to Mr. Spencer and again take his arm. We walk out of the library and to the foyer without me showing him my most prized possession, hidden secure in the library.

"Thank you for having me for tea. It was very considerate of you," says Mr. Spencer, taking hold of my hand and kissing the air above.

"Thank you for accepting my invitation. We must repeat the experience again soon," I say, pleasure filling my body.

"Goodbye Miss Fields," he says as he edges out the open door.

"Goodbye Mr. Spencer," I say, breathing out a sigh of longing as he walks down the sidewalk, away from the house and me.

WAKING UP, I LUXURIATE AMONG MY SILK SHEETS FOR A little longer before I force myself to get up and go about my tasks for the day.

When I finally pull myself from my bed, my body wanders naturally downstairs and through the rooms until I arrive at the library. But I stop. There, at the end of the room, the last pillar, the one holding my most precious possession, stands open.

My breath seizes in my lungs.

I run to the pillar where the hidden door is pulled into

the wood. My eyes must be deceiving me so I shove my hand along the shelf, checking all the deep shadows. But my dais is empty, my heart is gone.

Clutching my chest, I release a scream from my belly and sink to the floor, already tasting salt on my tongue as tears stream down my face. The only thoughts that manage to surface in my madness is that I no longer possess my heart.

LEAGUE OF CASANOVAS
PART TWO

The night presses down on me, weighing on my skin and clothes, making my movements slow and languid. I'm silent as I creep through the garden, booby trapped with thorned flowers and crunching stones. I don't like this part of the mission; sneaking up on sleeping dragons can't be on anyone's list of a good time. For my first time, I definitely don't want her to wake and find me stealing her treasure.

I've heard the stories back at headquarters. Some of the guys sit around on their evenings off competing with tales of bravery in the field. They talk of dragons rushing at them with knives, even swinging pans at their heads. I've never seen a dragon so fully provoked though, only minorly ruffled. That was scary enough. I can't imagine what would have happened if she had found me actually in the process of stealing her greatest treasure.

Creeping closer, I put my ear to the windowpane between the garden and the lair. I had stood for hours after leaving her, just at the edge of the garden, waiting for her to turn off all the lights, then giving another hour to ensure she was sound asleep before I began my slow and stealthy attack on the lair.

I slide my thin blade between the panes and flip the latch. Peeking through the heavy drapes, I make sure the room is clear and the house is silent before slipping through.

Quietly, making sure to step on the rugs instead of the squeaky floor boards, I step around the furniture and down the hallway to the library. The library is dark with heavy furniture and boarded windows blocking the little moonlight provided tonight. I move by touch and memory.

I remember walking three full strides straight from the doorway to the center of the room. This is followed by eight strides to the right and two more to the left and I'm there: the back-left pillar of the designed structural support of a large room.

Reaching out, my fingertips caress the unseen mahogany. Feeling the tiny ridged vertical lines, my mind recreates the picture of the day before when I was still seeking the location of the treasured weapon. The sunlight from the heavily secured windows had shed crystal diamonds on the deep red of the oriental runner which formed the path from door to desk, straight through the columns like a conquering emperor. Compared to the chairs and easy femininity of the parlor where I entered tonight, this room declares wars and masculinity with its heavy brown leather furniture and dark wood walls. Even trained as I am by the league, this room terrifies me. So close to such a terrible weapon, I cannot stop the shakes from coming on; can barely control them.

Starting at the base, I caress my fingers up the column seeking out, by touch, some small irregularity in the wood. I touch every square inch, leaving no room for errors; not this late in the mission. When my fingertips are about even with my hip bones, I feel a slight knot in the wood; small, maybe about the size of the pad of my pinky. Applying pressure in and around the knot, I feel a give in the wood, followed by a twinkling click.

Nervously I stand stock still, waiting to see if any alarm sounds or even if the dragon wakes. The knowledge of what they can and can't feel in relation to their treasure hoards is still a bit of a shaky area, even for my mentors. Some of the other League members are adamant that the connection is so strong as to wake a dragon from her slumber, but others say that their prolonged contact with such a dangerous weapon corrodes their connections to everything, so they do not immediately feel anything. Still I pause to hear if the dragon sleeping upstairs in her soft, fluffy bed full of pillows woke and would come rushing down the stairs to attack.

The lair remains silent. So I continue.

I grasp one of the ridges and wiggle it, trying to feel the give in the wood to see which way to tug. I pull away from the door where I entered the library.

The hard wood immediately folds into itself. Grabbing a small penlight from my bag, a single narrow shelf is revealed. There in the center, propped up as if on a dais lay a dark red beating ellipsoid with three cylindric vents protruding from the top, each pumping like an accordion into the mass, a breathing entity.

Glancing beneath the small shelf holding the beating heart, I see that the rest of the column below is not solid, but is in fact more of a wooden hole. Filling the bin with my light, I nearly gag at the sight of crushed hearts. How many men have suffered by her hands? I free myself to look away and regain my composure, to return my mind to the task at hand. I avoid dropping my gaze to the bin again. I refuse to be delayed in my mission.

From my bag I pull a pair of pure silver tongs and a small round canister. Lifting the lid from my silver container, I use the tongs to lightly grip the heart. The steady beating is soothing and grips me in a tantalizing peace, almost making me forget the task at hand. But I slowly transfer the heart from the dais to the canister and lock the lid in place before putting all my equipment back in my bag.

The task nearly complete, I hesitate, wondering if I should close the column so that the dragon does not immediately realize her loss or if I should leave it open, letting her know that such a dangerous weapon is no longer in her power.

In the end, I leave because there is nothing I can do. And there is no reason to endanger my own safety or that of other League members by further antagonizing the dragon.

RETURNING TO HEADQUARTERS, I TURN THE WEAPON OVER to my mentor. I watch as he opens the canister and again draws out the still beating heart. He places it on a new, smaller, more modest dais on a shelf of similar weapons. Each one is labelled with the name of the dragon who originally held the weapon, the date on which the weapon was confiscated and which member under took the task.

My mentor writes out the tag very neatly in clear penmanship:

Larina Fields
15 February 2034
Mark Spencer

His task completed, my mentor sits in an old armchair beside the fire and offers me three fingers of port. I swallow the amber liquid in one go and silently he refills my glass.

Watching the flames flicker in the grate, I say, "I was told how potent the weapon was and I could feel how drawn I was to its power, but I could never have imagined that level of destruction."

"You saw the dragon's hoard?" my mentor asks.

"Her bin was nearly filled with decomposing hearts."

"And this dragon was still young."

STEADY WORK

He can't sleep. He's too busy. He has to finish his masterpiece. Day and night he climbs up and down his ladder fetching paint, a new brush, a distant gaze. But he is never satisfied. Always, he must adjust his ladder, farther left or right, higher or lower. Always, he must shift his painting, waxing or waning, crackled or matted. Sometimes he paints it large and luminescent and some days he covers it in black, an empty canvas for him to stare at, to start anew.

He has to make a decision. He has to commit. Only then will his painting, will our moon, be static.

SOULMATES

Before homo sapiens, before Neanderthals, there lived the Androgynians. Molded from the earth by the gods, Androgynians possessed two faces like Janus and four arms after Hekatonkheir. As the gods sat on their thrones in the heavens, the Androgynians walked the earth wrapped in their wholeness of self. Displeased with this lack of worship from his progeny, Zeus loosed his lightning bolts, cleaving the Androgynians, doubling the population and destroying their wholeness.

SEATTLE, WASHINGTON

The overcast sky hung heavy with unreleased precipitation as Kevin hunched over a bowl of cereal, staring into the soggy essence. He watched the spoon travel from milk pond to mouth. His ears filled with compact guitar chords and manic drums, the earphones blocked out the morning prattle of his mother as she waited impatiently for her single serving coffee to percolate.

"Kevin," she called in exasperation. "Kevin!" She forced his name through the music and into his ears.

Pushing off one speaker, Kevin glanced up from his breakfast. "What?"

"I said," she sighed, drawing out her words, "you're going to be late. Don't you have a test in biology today?"

"I've got it covered," mumbled Kevin, slurping down the last mush from his bowl. Rising out of his chair, he shuffled from the table toward the door, dipping down to sling on his black backpack, patched with lyrics and sketches.

Opening the door wide, his mother snagged the loop on the backpack at the last moment, jerking him back a step. Turning his head to find the cause, Kevin caught his mother's kiss on his left cheek.

"No texting and driving. And no friends in the car. Good luck on your test," she said, ruffling Kevin's mop of brown hair.

"Yeah, yeah," said Kevin, wiping his cheek clean of any lipstick and flattening his hair back into place.

Released, he slipped out the door to the rusty red Honda in the driveway. He tossed his backpack over the gearshift and into the passenger seat. Removing the second headphone from his ear, he settled the speakers like a yoke where they beat against both sides of his neck, pumping his blood.

He drove fast, feeling the music thrum against his arteries as the tailpipe growled in chorus. The Honda produced only the distant rumbling of the cooling system, since the radio had broken before he learned to drive.

Turning onto Main Street, Kevin reached down to adjust the airflow on the defrost. The mornings were getting colder, and his breath obscured the windshield faster than the car could combat the condensation.

In this moment, with his eyes averted to the temperature settings, Kevin's hand over-adjusted the steering wheel by a few infinitesimal degrees. This inadvertent shift caused Kevin's beat-up old Honda to drive into a lamp post, making an accordion of the hood and a sudden silence of the music with the death of Kevin's body.

CHARLESTON, NORTH CAROLINA

Amy jerks awake for the fifth time in a week, bolting upright in her twin bed with pink paisley sheets, relieved to be in her bed and not the crashing car of her dream. Sweat dampens her brow and her sheets are nearly soaked through and twisted like ropes around her legs. Ignoring her bonds, Amy brushes her hair off her face as she gulps calming breaths to force the nightmare from her mind.

Equilibrium regained, she staggers out of bed and proceeds to dress for school before stumbling down to the kitchen and breakfast. The smell of pancakes and hot maple syrup fills the room and echoes in Amy's stomach as she enters to see her dad standing over the stove, flipping the cakes while her mom watches him over the rim of her orange juice.

"Morning, darling," calls her dad from behind a flying pancake.

"Morning," mumbles Amy into her arm as she slides the top half of her body along the island counter until she is beside her mother.

Her mother strokes the hair off Amy's face. "Feeling okay, sweetie?"

"Ugh. Do I have to go to school today?"

"When was your last panic attack?" asks her dad.

"But I don't want to go," says Amy into her arms, pretending that she can avoid the day if she doesn't look up.

"Amy," says her dad sharply, "you have to at least try. Stop giving up."

"Sweetie, please, just try to go to school. Maybe start cheering again? You can choose to be happy," says her mother.

"Ugh. You don't understand!" Amy rests her forehead directly on the countertop and covers her head with both forearms. "It doesn't mean anything!"

"We're trying, sweetie, but it will pass," says her mother.

"It's simple," says her father. "Just stop being sad and bummed all the time."

"Ugh," groans Amy.

"Well, then you'll just have to explain it to Dr Stanton. I don't know what to do with this constant mopiness anymore," says her mother, standing up to put her glass in the sink. Gathering her briefcase off the counter, her mother says, "You have an appointment after school today. Don't be late."

With this, her mother kisses both her and her father on the cheek before walking out of the house.

"Just understand. I don't want to do anything," groans Amy, stretching her long arms out along the counter. "Everything's empty."

"Let Dr Stanton help. He knows what he's doing," says her father, placing a stack of pancakes on a plate, smothering them with thick maple syrup, and pushing the edible tower toward her.

Amy pushes them around on her plate before her dad ends the discussion by dragging her to school, dragging her to therapy, dragging her through her old routine. She doesn't resist, but she doesn't participate either.

AMY SITS ON ONE SIDE OF A SMALL ROUND TABLE, HUNCHED, tracing the knots in the wood with chipped fingernails.

"Amy," says Dr Stanton. "Amy, do you want to tell me about your latest panic attack?"

Instead of answering, Amy switches her focus to her palms, tracing the jaggedness of her life lines, ignoring the overweight and overbearing man on the other side of the table.

"Did you manage to make it the entire car ride here today without a panic attack?" presses Dr Stanton.

"Ugh," says Amy, throwing open her arms. "It's not my fault!"

"I'm wondering, Amy," says Dr Stanton, "have you ever known anyone who was in a car accident?"

"No," she says.

"And this fear suddenly came out of nowhere all on its own?"

"I don't know, okay? All I know is I'm gonna die in a car."

"Did this fear precede your depression or come afterward?"

"I told you," she says. "I got a panic attack at school and since then I hate cars and I don't feel like me and I don't want to do anything."

"Why don't you want to do anything?"

"What's the point?" asks Amy.

"What do you think the point should be?" asks Dr Stanton.

"Ugh!"

Adjusting his glasses, Dr Stanton says, "Can you describe this 'sadness' that you feel?"

"I just feel empty, okay?" Amy spreads her fingers wide against the tabletop. "I feel like I died and I don't have the energy to go through these stupid motions."

"What makes these motions of living 'stupid'?"

"It just is, okay? I don't want to do anything," says Amy, throwing her arms out in crucifixion.

"I see," says Dr Stanton, pulling out a notepad and pen. "I'm going to write you a prescription. It should help with the anxiety and combat the depression. If that doesn't work, come back and see me."

Dr Stanton gives the slip to Amy, effectively dismissing her from the appointment. She takes the prescription and shuffles from the room, not bothering to say thanks or goodbye.

Amy sees her future as empty. She thinks, *what's the point?*

SOULMATES AGAIN

Kathy lay in bed staring up at the ceiling. How is it that all hotel ceilings look alike? Same dirty colors and standard light fixtures dulled with dust and bugs.

"How much time do you have left?" asks Mark.

Kathy checks her wristwatch on the bedside table. "About ten minutes," she says rolling back over to curl across Mark's bare chest.

Instead of putting his arm around her and pulling her close, Mark pulls away and sits at the edge of the bed with his back to her.

"What's wrong?" asks Kathy, rubbing Mark's back.

Still he doesn't turn toward her. "I hate this. These few hours, hiding away. It isn't fair and it isn't right."

"I know. What do you want me to do though? I can't walk away from my kids."

"So you're willing to live this lie? What about me? You're expecting me to just survive on the few scraps you manage to throw me?"

"No, of course not."

"So you expect me to some day walk away so I can finally have a family? You know I want children, children with you. Or do you want to see each other on the side for the rest of our lives? Do you want me to subject my hypothetical wife to that?" Mark steps away from Kathy's stroking hand and pulls his pants on.

"I guess I haven't thought about that yet. I've just been enjoying the time we do have together," says Kathy, moving to the spot Mark vacated, the sheet wrapped around her.

"I think you need to consider what you want from this and make a decision."

Kathy tugs the sheet with her as she stands and walks over to Mark. Wrapping herself around him, she whispers into his shoulder, "I love you."

Finally embracing her, Mark asks, "Why didn't you wait for me?"

"I was afraid you weren't coming," says Kathy, squeezing him tighter, afraid to let go now that she has found him. "Afraid you, maybe, didn't even exist."

"But I do."

KATHY IS CHOPPING VEGETABLES FOR THE PASTA WHEN Brian throws an envelope down on the counter next to her.

"Why did you do it?"

"Do what?" asks Kathy, not looking up from the chopping board, making the cubes mince.

"Cheat." He taps a corner of the envelope as if to move it closer to her. "I have pictures."

"What do you want me to say?" asks Kathy, cautiously setting down the knife, but still not turning to face Brian, not ready to look at her prison.

"I want you to tell me exactly why you went outside our

marriage. Why you specifically broke the vows you said before God. Did you even consider the kids?"

"Of course I considered the kids!" Kathy swings around to face Brian.

"And?" Brian's face is a mash of disgust.

"Why do you think I'm still here? Still making dinner, packing lunches, doing laundry. I'm doing this for them. Everything I do is for them."

"Even having an affair is for them?" Brian grabs the envelope from the counter and holds it up inches from her face, forcing her to flinch away.

"No, that I did for me."

"You're selfish. You always have been." Brian walks over to the fridge and pulls out a beer.

"Oh yeah, so selfish. Giving up school when I got knocked up and doing everything for you all these years. So selfish of me." Kathy throws up her hands in mock horror.

"Yes, selfish. You're jeopardizing this family. You. This is your fault."

"No, I don't think it is," says Kathy quietly.

Brian opens the beer and takes a long pull. "Stop seeing whatever-his-name-is. Or the kids will find out and you'll never see them again," he says, holding up the envelope threateningly.

As Brian steps out the back door, Kathy brushes away the tension in her face, trying to brush away the marriage she settled for instead of waiting, and whispers, "I wish I had never met you."

THE WIND'S LOVE

The wind howls because he cannot stay with her.

Many years ago there was a beautiful woman and the wind fell in love. He would brush her hair and fan out her skirts, dancing her through meadows. And she loved him in return, following him across all terrains.

Time passed and the wind's beloved aged, no longer able to keep up with his rovings. The wind begged for the sun's assistance to turn his love into a bird, but the sun simply looked the other way.

The wind begged the earth instead and the earth grew up around the woman, encasing her in a mountain so she could live forever.

The earth's gift was both a blessing and a curse. The wind's love lived on, yet they could no longer frolic as they once did. The wind began to howl, mourning his loss.

He howls still, only able to caress his love in passing. There are never enough of those moments.

THE WIND HOWLS BECAUSE HE CANNOT STAY WITH HER.

She used to be a beautiful woman, free to roam and frolic. She once loved the wind who now violently strokes her body. But that was when they would play and dance together. Before the earth trapped her in this mountain and the wind left her, only to caress her at his own whim and then move on, inconsistent in his passion.

Now her once full curves are eroding from his touch, changing her face, shaping her into who he wants her to be. Caged in his love, unable to roam.

And still he howls. And still she sits.

A WATERFALL

A boy in the village was hungry all the time, so he would eat and eat. Soon he grew bigger than all the other boys and they would make fun of him, shunning him. He comforted himself with more food, until he grew so big that he towered over everyone in his village, even the grown men.

Eventually, he was so big that he could plow a field in a few strides and scythe an entire meadow in an afternoon. But his size also made him clumsy. He once sat down and crushed a neighbor's goat. He would sleep outside because no bed could contain him and would roll too far, flattening entire huts.

Soon the villagers became a mob and drove him away. They said he cost too much in food and damage to outweigh the help he was in the field. They said that they would rather work harder than have him around.

So he went off to a snug little valley where he curled up and cried. He cried because he was clumsy and because he was too big and because he lost his family. He cried because he was lonely. He cried himself to sleep, but even in dreams his tears flowed.

Days and seasons passed without his waking as earth piled up against him, over his shoulders and arms; piled over his face until there was nothing left, until he was but a mountain of dirt with a waterfall of tears, waiting for somebody to come, to brush away his sadness and welcome him into their arms. But his tears were the only part of him rushing to meet the world, carrying his sorrows to the ends of the earth.

THE STAR CHRONICLES

ANANSI'S LOSS

Anansi followed in her mother's and her grandmother's footsteps. She gathered herbs by moonlight, collected roots, and crushed seeds, making cures and poultices for her people. They came to her and she healed them.

By her side was Wahkan, partner for her life. Wahkan was a great warrior and claimed many hunting grounds for his people. Their blood enemy to the north, the Omnootaun, often tried to steal their lands and their women, but Wahkan fought them off time and again.

It was in one of these skirmishes that Wahkan was injured and called upon Anansi to tend his wounds. Anansi lay Wahkan out under the sky beside the blessed fire which she fanned over his injuries, praying to the land and the ancestors to heal Wahkan's body.

When Wahkan again opened his eyes, he was looking up at Nordstern who was looking back. Nordstern began to tell Wahkan stories to speed his healing. Wahkan began to spend his days with Nordstern's whispers and his nights in Nordstern's rays, ignoring Anansi and moving to a new sleeping place.

The tribe was proud to hold a star lover and asked Wahkan to counsel their chief and elders. Anansi continued to attend the tribe meetings, but spoke less with each passing night as she watched Wahkan fall ever deeper in love with his star.

THE STAR CHRONICLES

THE GIFT OF LIGHT

When the stars still held the blossom of youth, the Omnootaun, the Fireless People, lived at the edge of the wood. The Omnootaun had once hunted the dense center teeming with animals, but their lands were stolen by Wahkan, leader of their enemy tribe.

None of the Omnootaun had ever been beloved by any star, while Wahkan was rewarded for his treachery with such love. The Fireless People watched as Wahkan, with his star, led his tribe to gain more and more of the forest.

Nearly in the plains, the Omnootaun came upon Anansi as she searched for herbs. They pressed her into helping them achieve revenge against Wahkan.

That night, Anansi prepared a sacred fire laced with hemlock, and called on her ancestors to avenge their family name. The Omnootaun breathed in the smoke and their souls slipped out, transforming into flies with tiny stars strapped to their backs. As the stars shone bright against the sky, the Omnootaun flew among them, using their new lights to give false messages to the Wahkan and neighboring star lovers.

Before Earth or Moon could intervene, fighting broke out among the tribes and no one trusted the stars anymore.

No longer following the stars, the tribes decided to build new homes that would not move. They no longer followed their lovers across the sky, but looked down instead, to the earth.

When next the moon was hiding, the Omnootaun returned to Anansi, ready to relinquish their new figures for their human shapes, but their bodies were nowhere to be found. Anansi had gone to the leader of her tribe and shown that she had burned the bodies of their rivals. Anansi's tribe, seeing such skill, venerated her power, believing her knowledge must be greater than the stars, who had caused such chaos among the tribes.

Generations later, the Omnootaun continue on as fireflies, unable to return to their bodies, still working against the stars who never chose them, and delivering incoherent messages on summer nights. The stars may now only watch as their light burns on, forlorn in the solitude of unrequited love.

ACKNOWLEDGEMENTS

Gratitude to the editors of the following anthologies in which pages these fables first appeared, sometimes in a different form:

Blazo, Alby. "How Worms Came Into Existence." *A New Beginning*, Women Who Write, Melbourne, Melbourne, VIC, 2017, pp. 103–104.

Blazo, Alby. "League of Casanovas." *Heroes & Villains*, MelbourneWriters-Group, Melbourne, VIC, 2018, pp. 268–275.

Blazo, Alby. "Loveless Legend of the Mainz Parrots." *The Ties That Bind*, Melbourne Writers Social Group, Melbourne, VIC, 2017, pp. 16–17.

Blazo, Alby. "Why Whales Jump." *A Pod of Tales*, Love, Luna Press, Grand Rapids, MI, 2021, pp. 44–45.

ABOUT THE AUTHOR

Alby Blazo is a grant award winning author best known for micro-fables of an Aesopian nature and tightly-packed poetry. She often writes about themes of home, family and loss. When not writing, Alby can most often be found in her garden or admiring her cats.

Thank you for reading. If you enjoyed this collection of fables, please consider leaving a review.

BONUS CONTENT

THE COLLAPSE

Arthur looks out from beneath his towel, still covering his head. He especially doesn't stand up from his crouch, not until he is assured of his safety.

"Thank goodness you figured it out in time. We didn't think you would make it," says the man standing over him.

He's quite tall and Arthur does not like his current position, embarrassing himself in front of such an authoritative looking man. Arthur quickly readjusts his position, draping his towel around his neck and aping the man.

"What do you mean 'make it'? Where am I?" asks Arthur.

"Well, on board the Star Canoe as we promised after Mars, of course. Why, you didn't want us to leave you on Earth, did you?"

Arthur isn't sure if the man is actually serious in his concern or merely making fun of him. People often make fun of him.

"With the sky crashing down on me? Of course not!" Arthur pulls his shirt down over his belly a bit more.

"Technically speaking, your sky wasn't crashing. But that

isn't important," says the man, walking off down one of the many hallways.

Arthur watches him walk away before stumbling after him. His legs aren't quite steady yet. "What do you mean, not important? It feels pretty important to me! After all, I'm the one that was just nearly squashed."

"Are you still focused on that? You're not even the tiniest bit incinerated. Not everyone from your planet can say the same."

"Wait, what happened to everyone else?"

The hallway they're walking down is pocked with what look like port windows, tiny and smudged, but clearly displaying a floating dust cloud.

"They died obviously. No one can survive the collapse of their atmosphere. You're lucky you figured out the password." The man gestures Arthur into a gleaming white broom cupboard with a small black triangle at shoulder level.

"No, I didn't." Arthur doesn't step into said broom cupboard. He's not about to let this strange space man shove him into the equivalent of a junior high locker on some weird spaceship, if that's really even where he is.

"Don't be silly. Of course you did. We wouldn't have been able to pick you up if you hadn't," says the man, manhandling Arthur into the cupboard.

"I don't know anything about a password." Arthur nearly falls face first into the triangle. "What was the password anyway?"

"If you don't know it, I can't tell you." The man stops to consider Arthur, showing uncertainty for the first time. At the same time the triangle shoots out from the wall on a snake hose and sniffs Arthur all over. "Maybe we shouldn't have saved you then."

"Of course you should have saved me!" Arthur tries to fight off the sniffing triangle. "I was thinking about hiding beneath the canoe around the back of my house when you showed up. Who knows if that bit of tin would have saved me!"

"So you hadn't figured it out then. You were just thinking a regular canoe in your own home. The commander is not going to like this at all." The triangle finally retreats into the wall and the space man continues to walk down the hall with hurried strides.

"You can't kick me out now over some silly little password." Arthur trails behind, casting nervous glances at the cloud outside.

"Why not? It's not like you earned your place here, now did you?"

"Because that's not very humane for one thing!"

"Then it's a good thing neither of us are human."

"I beg your pardon! I am a full-blood male homo sapien, thank you very much!" Arthur pulls down the hem of his shirt to make sure his belly isn't sticking out.

The space man turns around abruptly, forcing Arthur to skid to a halt. "I don't understand this classification that you people have given yourselves. Your entire tree is wrong. You're crazier than a bunch of Mirhuffs if you think you're descended from apes. What a stupid idea," he says, shaking in his head.

"A bunch of Mirhuffs? What are you talking about?" Arthur is even more confused now, trying to follow the man as he starts walking again.

He looks longingly behind him, it's not home, but it was the closest thing. He missed those backward folks he always despised, they were ignorant, but at least he understood what they were talking about. Most of the time, at least.

"Captain, as you requested." The space man pushes through a pair of swinging doors which slam back and hit Arthur in the face.

He was never very good at timing these sorts of things, or making decent, non-embarrassing, entrances.

"How many rescues did we collect?" asks the man who Arthur can only suppose is the captain, especially since he has a big badge that reads 'captain'.

"Just the one, Captain. But there seems to have been a mistake."

"What do you mean, mistake?" The captain grips his armrests.

"He didn't know the password."

"What do you mean, he didn't know the password? How did he beam on board if he didn't have the password?"

"He accidentally thought it at just the right moment. Exceedingly lucky for him," says the space man.

Throughout this entire exchange Arthur half pays attention, as the topic does concern him, but he's also fascinated by the room which is not at all what he thought a spaceship would look like. Not that he'd spent any time imagining what it would be like aboard a spaceship, always having much more practical and realistic items to contemplate. The entire interior continues in the same gleaming white, with milky computer screens set in them, and a vertical wrought-iron spiral staircase in the center decorated with potted ferns. The room is a bit modern for Arthur's taste, but not the worst place he could have ended up he supposed.

"Rescue," says the captain. "Rescue!"

The space man beside Arthur elbows him, making Arthur realize that he must be being addressed. "Yes, uh, Captain?"

"I'm Captain Hemi. You've already met Lieutenant Kiri."

"Sort of, well no, not really. We kind of skipped the introduction portion." Arthur checks the hem of his shirt.

"What are you called?" Captain Hemi shoots his lieutenant a disapproving look.

"Arthur."

"Now Arthur, as I'm sure Lieutenant Kiri has explained, you don't really belong here if you didn't figure out the password for yourself."

"But I did manage to get aboard and that has to count for something, right?" Arthur glances at Lieutenant Kiri in the faint hope that he might support him in this argument, but the Lieutenant is slipping out through a wall panel.

"As a technicality, I suppose. But then that still isn't really fair to the rest of your population who died because they didn't find the clue either."

"What clue? Was there some tablet that we missed that said, 'Should the world begin to end, think 'Canoe' and you'll be saved'?"

"Of course, not. Tablets break. No, our method was much better, an oral history. Although at some point they usually do write it down somewhere."

"Uh, no. I must have missed that day in history class," says Arthur as Lieutenant Kiri re-enters through the wall panel with a silver tea cart covered in delicate china cups and saucers as well as a plate of what appears to be cucumber sandwiches.

"Really? They usually leave the clues all over the place." Captain Hemi accepts a cup of tea. "Two lumps please," he says to the Lieutenant, who pulls out miniature tongs and plonks the sugar cubes into the captain's cup.

"Well we didn't find any. I told you, you got this all wrong. Our ancestors were primitive, lived in caves, made a few pots, that's it. They weren't as intelligent as us, not by a long shot." Arthur waves his hands across his chest to refuse the cup of tea the Lieutenant offers.

"I think you just weren't smart enough to look in the right places. I mean, they weren't trying to communicate with their neighbor the next planet over. They were sending a message to a fledgling civilization thousands of years in the future," says the captain.

Lieutenant Kiri presses the china cup into Arthur's face.

"I don't want any bloody tea! We never got a message! Or a clue! Or anything for that matter. I don't remember any of this."

Lieutenant Kiri continues to shove the tea into Arthur's hands until he accepts, not being able to think of any other way to express his lack of desire for the beverage in any way other than vocally and physically.

"Didn't you ever hear stories about where you came from or what would happen after your Earth died? Any texts? Or pictures? Sometimes these things get muddled in the retelling."

"The only stories are the myths which obviously aren't true since they involve gods."

"You're hurtling through space in a spaceship and you think myths aren't real? Ever considered the fact that the gods may just be a more advanced species than you? Or are you really that conceited?" Lieutenant Kiri interjected.

"We were very clear that your atmosphere would collapse and that the Canoe would come and sail you away. I'm not sure how we could have prepared you any better. The ones we left on your planet promised to tell the story often," says Captain Hemi.

"Now that you mention it," Arthur admitted. "There is an old myth that my gran used to tell about a canoe appearing on the horizon when humans were being crushed. Or something like that."

"A myth! What did you think happened to Mars? How do you think you migrated from Mars to Earth? Magic? This is real history!"

"Wait, you mean this happened? Before?"

"Countless times. That's why we keep hopping planets.

They can only take a few dozen cycles of civilization before they give out."

"That can't be right. The Earth isn't even that old and we're the only civilization. Before us there were cavemen and dinosaurs."

"Your education system really failed you, didn't it?"

"Then I guess I didn't figure it out, but no one else did either. You can't punish me for that."

"You're making a lot of assumptions there." Captain Hemi looks Arthur over from head to toe. Arthur wishes he wasn't wearing his jeans with the mustard stain. "But then I suppose we do need a historian from whom we can extract all the details of what life on your planet was like. And you're the only one to actually have survived. We'll have to speak with HR about how to improve our coding system to change that for next time. You can stay."

"Yes," says Arthur, shooting his fist into the air.

www.ingramcontent.com/pod-product-compliance
Lightning Source LLC
Chambersburg PA
CBHW010643190726
48289CB00009B/2841

* 9 7 8 1 7 3 6 3 5 3 4 7 9 *